At Issue

Student Loans

Other Books in the At Issue Series

Are Graphic Music Lyrics Harmful?

Bilingual Education

Caffeine

Can Diets Be Harmful?

Childhood Obesity

Corporate Corruption

Does the Internet Increase Anxiety?

Foodborne Outbreaks

Foreign Oil Dependence

How Valuable Is a College Degree?

Immigration Reform

Invasive Species

The Olympics

Superbugs

Superfoods

Voter Fraud

What Is the Impact of Green Practices?

What Should We Eat?

At Issue

Student Loans

Noël Merino, Book Editor

GREENHAVEN PRESS
A part of Gale, Cengage Learning

GALE
CENGAGE Learning·

Farmington Hills, Mich • San Francisco • New York • Waterville, Maine
Meriden, Conn • Mason, Ohio • Chicago

Judy Galens, *Manager, Frontlist Acquisitions*

© 2016 Greenhaven Press, a part of Gale, Cengage Learning.

Gale and Greenhaven Press are registered trademarks used herein under license.

For more information, contact:
Greenhaven Press
27500 Drake Rd.
Farmington Hills, MI 48331-3535
Or you can visit our Internet site at gale.cengage.com

For product information and technology assistance, contact us at

Gale Customer Support, 1-800-877-4253
For permission to use material from this text or product, submit all requests online at www.cengage.com/permissions.

Further permissions questions can be e-mailed to permissionrequest@cengage.com.

Articles in Greenhaven Press anthologies are often edited for length to meet page requirements. In addition, original titles of these works are changed to clearly present the main thesis and to explicitly indicate the author's opinion. Every effort is made to ensure that Greenhaven Press accurately reflects the original intent of the authors. Every effort has been made to trace the owners of copyrighted material.

Cover photograph copyright © Todd Davidson/Illustration Works/Corbis.

LIBRARY OF CONGRESS CATALOGING-IN-PUBLICATION DATA

Student loans / Noël Merino, Book Editor.
    pages cm. -- (At issue)
Includes bibliographical references and index.
ISBN 978-0-7377-7410-8 (hardcover) -- ISBN 978-0-7377-7411-5 (pbk.)
1. Student loans--United States--Juvenile literature. 2. Student loans--Government policy--United States--Juvenile literature. I. Merino, Noël.
LB2340.2.S8464 2016
378.3'62--dc23
                        2015028557

Printed in Mexico
1 2 3 4 5 6 7 19 18 17 16

Contents

Introduction

There is no debate that the amount of student loans has risen in the past couple decades, even after factoring in the role of inflation. That fact in itself, however, does not indicate there is a problem. In fact, there is widespread disagreement about the extent to which the current student loan situation constitutes a social crisis. On the one hand, students are graduating (or not) with unprecedented levels of student loan debt. On the other hand, student loans have made college accessible for many students who may not have been able to finance their education without going into debt.

The Institute for College Access & Success (TICAS) reported that in 2013, 69 percent of graduating seniors at public and private nonprofit colleges had student loan debt (private for-profit colleges were not included in the report due to a lack of access to student loan debt data at such colleges). About one-fifth of all the student loan debt was from private loans, with the bulk coming from federal student loans. The average amount owed at graduation for both federal and private loans was $28,400. The amount of debt varied by state and by school.

The states that graduated students with the highest amount of debt were largely in the Northeast and Midwest. New Hampshire tops the list, with average student loan debt at graduation of $32,795. Also in the top ten, in descending order, are Delaware, Pennsylvania, Rhode Island, Minnesota, Connecticut, Maine, Michigan, Iowa, and South Carolina. At the other end, New Mexico had college graduates with the lowest amount of student loan debt, with an average of $18,656. Other low-debt states concentrated in the West and South, in order of ascending debt, were California, Nevada, District of Columbia, Oklahoma, Arizona, Utah, Hawaii, Wyoming, and Louisiana.

Another factor that varied for the class of 2013 by state was the percentage of students graduating with debt. Whereas 76 percent of New Hampshire college graduates had student loan debt, only 43 percent of graduating seniors in Nevada had taken out student loans.

Student loan debt levels also vary greatly according to college. Factors such as tuition, cost of living in the college area, demographics of classmates, the availability of grants and scholarships, and the number of out-of-state students (at public colleges) affect the cost of attendance. Public colleges tend to have lower tuition costs than private nonprofit colleges, but cost of attendance can often be greatly reduced by scholarships and grants at private nonprofit colleges.

TICAS compiled lists of colleges with notably high levels of student loan debt among graduates utilizing the data available. Among public colleges, with annual tuition and fees ranging from $6,100 to $16,600, were four University of Pittsburgh campuses, Pennsylvania State University, University of Maine, University of West Alabama, Texas Southern University, Kentucky State University, Citadel Military College of South Carolina, and ten others. These high-debt public colleges had graduates with student loan debt averaging from $33,950 to $48,850.

Among private nonprofit colleges, with annual tuition and fees ranging from $24,550 to $41,500, were Abilene Christian University, Pacific Union College, Quinnipiac University, Saint Anselm College, University of Hartford, University of the Sciences, Utica College, and Wheelock College, and twelve others. College graduates from these private nonprofit colleges had average debt ranging from $41,750 to $71,350.

Colleges with notably low levels of student loan debt— with average graduating debt under $11,200—included the private nonprofits Princeton University and Howard University, as well as three campuses in the public California State

University system and four campuses in the public CUNY (City University of New York) system.

There is controversy about student loans because some say that the student loan debt levels have gotten too high, but others claim that the benefits of a college degree outweigh this burden. A 2013 poll conducted by Harstad Strategic Research found that about half of eighteen to thirty-one year-olds worry about repaying student loan debt. There is no easy solution, however. When polled in 2011 by Rasmussen Reports, two-thirds of Americans opposed forgiveness of all student loans. In *At Issue: Student Loans* the authors of the various viewpoints illustrate the wide-ranging opinions that exist on the matter of student loans and demonstrate the likelihood of this being a controversial social issue for some time to come.

Student Loans and Default Rates Have Increased in Recent Years

National Center for Education Statistics, US Department of Education

The National Center for Education Statistics, within the US Department of Education, is the primary federal entity for collecting and analyzing data related to education.

Undergraduate tuition and fees have increased in recent years, as has the average student loan debt. Among students who entered the repayment phase on their student loans in 2011, 13.7 percent had defaulted by 2013. The default rate was highest at two-year public institutions (20.6 percent) and lowest at four-year private nonprofit institutions (7 percent).

Title IV of the Higher Education Act of 1965 authorized several student financial assistance programs—including federal grants, loans, and work study—to help offset the cost of attending a postsecondary institution. The largest federal loan program is the William D. Ford Federal Direct Loan program; the federal government is the lender for this program. Interest on the loans made under the Direct Loan program may be subsidized, based on need, while the student is in school. Most loans are payable over 10 years, beginning 6 months after the student leaves the institution, either by completing the program or by leaving prior to completion.

National Center for Education Statistics, US Department of Education, "Student Loan Volume and Default Rates," pp. 190–193 in *The Condition of Education 2014*, May 2014. Courtesy of nces.ed.gov.

College Tuition and Students

Average undergraduate tuition and fees for full-time students across all degree-granting postsecondary institutions in 2011–12 were $10,300 in constant 2012–13 dollars—a 46 percent increase over 2000–01 ($7,100). Among 4-year institutions, tuition and fees at public institutions had the largest percentage increase (69 percent, from $4,600 to $7,800) during this period; however, the largest dollar amount increase was at private nonprofit institutions ($7,200 increase, from $20,900 to $28,100). The smallest change among 4-year institutions was at private for-profit institutions (1 percent higher in 2011–12 than in 2000–01, $13,900 vs. $13,800). Among 2-year institutions, the largest percentage increase in tuition and fees during this period occurred at private nonprofit institutions (55 percent, from $9,200 to $14,300), while the smallest increase in tuition and fees occurred at private for-profit institutions (8 percent, from $13,100 to $14,200).

Of the 4.7 million students who entered the repayment phase on their student loans in FY 2011, some 476,000, or 10.0 percent, had defaulted before the end of FY 2012.

In 2011–12, average undergraduate tuition and fees at 4-year degree-granting postsecondary institutions were $13,800 in 2011–12 (in constant 2012–13 dollars). Average in-state tuition and fees were lowest at public 4-year institutions ($7,800), followed by private for-profit 4-year institutions ($13,900) and private nonprofit 4-year institutions ($28,100). At 2-year degree-granting postsecondary institutions, average undergraduate tuition and fees were $3,300. Average in-state tuition and fees were lowest at public 2-year institutions ($2,700), followed by private for-profit 2-year institutions ($14,200) and private nonprofit 2-year institutions ($14,300).

In 2011–12, some 51 percent of first-time, full-time undergraduate students enrolled in student aid programs received student loans. Between 2000–01 and 2011–12, the overall percentage of students receiving loan aid increased by 11 percentage points. During this period, the percentage of students receiving loan aid increased at all types of institutions, with the largest increase among 4-year institutions occurring at private for-profit institutions (from 58 to 83 percent) and the largest increase among 2-year institutions occurring at private nonprofit institutions (from 49 to 66 percent).

Average annual student loan amounts for first-time, fulltime undergraduate students enrolled in student aid programs also increased between 2000–01 and 2011–12, from $5,000 to $6,800, after adjusting for inflation (a 36 percent increase). Average loan amounts were higher in 2011–12 than in 2000–01 for all types of institutions. Among 4-year institutions, the largest percentage increase in average loan amount was at public institutions (52 percent, from $4,200 to $6,500), while the smallest percentage change was at private for-profit institutions (10 percent higher, from $7,600 to $8,400). In 2011–12, inflation-adjusted average annual student loan amounts were highest at private for-profit 4-year institutions ($8,400) and lowest at public 2-year institutions ($4,800). Among 2-year institutions, the largest percentage increase in average loan amount during this period was at public institutions (52 percent, from $3,200 to $4,800), while the smallest change was at private for-profit institutions (7 percent higher, from $7,100 to $7,600).

Student Loan Default

Approximately 4.7 million students entered the repayment phase of their student loans in fiscal year (FY) 2011, meaning that their student loans became due between October 1, 2010, and September 30, 2011. The percentage of students who entered repayment on their loans in FY 2011 and defaulted prior to the end of the next fiscal year is the 2-year cohort default rate. Of the 4.7 million students who entered the repayment phase on their student loans in FY 2011, some 476,000, or 10.0 percent, had defaulted before the end of FY 2012. For students in the Direct Loan Program or the Federal Family Education Loan (FFEL) program, default occurs when a payment has not been made for 270 days.

The default rate for students in the FY 2011 cohort was 8.2 percent at 4-year degree-granting postsecondary institutions and 14.6 percent at 2-year degree-granting postsecondary institutions. The default rate for the FY 2011 cohort was highest at public 2-year institutions (15.0 percent). The lowest default rate was for students at private nonprofit 4-year institutions (5.1 percent).

Across all institutions, the overall default rate for the FY 2011 cohort (10.0 percent) was higher than the rates for the FY 2010 (9.1 percent) and FY 2009 (8.8 percent) cohorts. The largest percentage point increase in default rates from FY 2009 to FY 2011 was at public 2-year institutions (from 11.9 to 15.0 percent). During this period, the largest percentage point decrease occurred at private for-profit 4-year institutions (from 15.4 to 13.4 percent).

Why You Might Be Paying Student Loans Until You Retire

Sophie Quinton

Sophie Quinton covers higher education and economic development as a staff correspondent at the National Journal.

Student loan debt has risen across every age group over the last ten years. Many borrowers are not paying off their debt fast enough to reduce the total amount that they owe and others are falling into delinquency and default because of their inability to pay.

Rosemary Anderson has a master's degree, a good job at the University of California (Santa Cruz), and student loans that she could be paying off until she's 81.

The Rise in Student Loan Debt

Anderson, who is 57, told her complicated story at a recent Senate Aging Committee hearing (she's previously appeared on the *CBS Evening News*). She first enrolled in college in her thirties. Over the past two decades, her personal finances have been eroded by illness, divorce, the cost of raising two children, the housing bust, and the economic downturn. She hasn't been able to afford payments on her loans for nearly eight years.

Some 3 percent of U.S. households that are headed by a senior citizen now hold federal student debt, mostly debt they took on to finance their own educations, according to a new report from the Government Accountability Office [GAO], an independent agency. "As the baby boomers continue to move into retirement, the number of older Americans with defaulted loans will only continue to increase," the report warned.

Student debt has risen across every age group over the past decade, according to a Federal Reserve Bank of New York analysis of credit report data. . . . "There are more people attending college, more people taking out loans, and more people taking out a higher dollar amount of loans," says Matthew Ward, associate director of media relations at the New York Fed.

There's currently no way to get rid of federal student debt other than paying off the loans.

While some borrowers are paying off their debts just fine, overall they're adding debt faster than they're shedding it, the New York Fed found. Between 2005 and 2011, borrowers under age 50 added more debt on average than they paid off. "Only those 60 and older are paying down (or otherwise lowering) their student debt, on average," senior economists Meta Brown and Donghoon Lee said in an email.

Brown and Lee think the data suggest three things. First, Americans are taking out loans throughout their lives to finance education for themselves and for their children. Second, some borrowers aren't paying enough each month to reduce the total balance they owe. And third, some borrowers are falling into delinquency and default.

After graduate school, Anderson had a mess of federal and private, subsidized and unsubsidized loans, which she decided to consolidate. The interest rate on the packaged loans, 8.25

percent, didn't seem like a big deal at the time. Then her financial situation changed. "It was like the perfect storm," she told *National Journal*.

Eliminating Student Loan Debt

There's currently no way to get rid of federal student debt other than paying off the loans. When borrowers stop making payments, the loan just sits there, accumulating fees and interest. After a borrower defaults, if she still does nothing, the government can sue, call in a debt collection agency, take a cut of her wages, or start taking money out of her tax refunds or monthly benefits like Social Security.

Anderson's lucky: She never defaulted. If she had, her debt load would likely be even larger, and her chances of paying it off even smaller. About 12 percent of the federal loans held by people ages 25 to 49 are already in default, according to the GAO report.

She's also lucky she graduated. College dropouts with student loans land in the worst situation of all: They have debt but no degree to help them access better-paying jobs. Many people in this situation are low-income, minority, or first-generation college students.

At least in theory, it's becoming easier for borrowers to manage their debt. Borrowers can ask the Education Department to adjust their loan payments according to their income, for example. Under income-driven repayment plans, the government will forgive remaining debt after 20 or 25 years.

But not enough people know that those options exist. And some of the repayment possibilities are better suited to a traditional college student—the young person who just completed a four-year degree—than to older people with a complicated loan history, like Anderson. "You can say all these resources are around and you have all these options, but they don't fit every single person," she says.

3

Increased Student Loan Debt Is Not a Big Problem

Beth Akers and Matthew M. Chingos

Beth Akers is a fellow in the Brookings Institution's Brown Center on Education Policy and Matthew M. Chingos is a senior fellow at the Brookings Institution and research director of its Brown Center on Education Policy.

Although student loan debt has increased in the past decade, it is still the case that the economic return on a college education in terms of increased earnings outweighs both the short-term and long-term burdens of paying off the debt incurred in getting a college degree.

When the total balance of outstanding student debt passed the $1 trillion mark two years ago [2012], it prompted many to question whether the student lending market was headed for a crisis, with many students unable to repay their loans and taxpayers being forced to foot the bill. There is clear evidence that the number of students taking on debt to pay for tuition, fees, and living expenses while in college has been increasing and that debt burdens have been growing. Over the last 20 years, inflation-adjusted published tuition and fees have more than doubled at four-year public institutions, and have increased by more than 50 percent at private four-year and public two-year colleges.

Beth Akers and Matthew M. Chingos, "Is a Student Loan Crisis on the Horizon?," Brown Center on Education Policy at Brookings, June 2014, pp. 3–4, 13–18. brookings.edu.

The Growth in Student Loan Debt

Media reports of students with large debts—often in excess of $100,000—have garnered a great deal of public attention. However, the debt picture for the typical college graduate is not so dire. For example, bachelor's degree recipients in 2011–12 who took out student loans accumulated an average debt load of approximately $26,000 ($25,000 at public institutions, and $29,900 at private, nonprofit institutions). However, current debt levels represent substantial increases over previous levels, with debt per borrower 20 percent higher in inflation-adjusted terms in 2011–12 than it was ten years prior. At the same time, extremely high debt levels remain quite rare: in 2012, only four percent of student loan balances were greater than $100,000.

To the extent that borrowers are using debt as a tool to finance investments in human capital that pay off through higher wages in the future, increases in debt may simply be a benign symptom of increasing expenditure on higher education.

And despite the recent recession, the significant economic return to college education continues to grow, implying that many of these loans are financing sound investments. In 2011, college graduates between the ages of 23 and 25 earned $12,000 more per year, on average, than high school graduates in the same age group, and had employment rates 20 percentage points higher. Over the last 30 years, the increase in lifetime earnings associated with earning a bachelor's degree has grown by 75 percent, while costs have grown by 50 percent. There is also an earnings premium associated with attending college and earning an associate's degree or no degree at all, although it is not as large. These economic benefits accrue to individuals, but also to society, in the form of increased tax revenue, improved health, and higher levels of civic participation.

Consequently, it is not obvious that the growth in debt is problematic. Commentators have expressed concerns that increasing education debt loads are making it more difficult for borrowers to start families, buy houses, and save for retirement. But these concerns rest on an evidence base that is insufficient to determine what these increases in debt mean for the financial well-being of borrowers and for the health of the overall student lending market. . . .

Measuring the Burden of Student Loan Debt

The growth in student loan debt is often discussed as a problem in and of itself. However, to the extent that borrowers are using debt as a tool to finance investments in human capital that pay off through higher wages in the future, increases in debt may simply be a benign symptom of increasing expenditure on higher education. This would be the case if the observed increases in borrowing occurred in tandem with improvements in financial well-being. On the contrary, if these expenditures were spent in ways that don't pay dividends in the future, then the observed growth in debt may indicate problems for the financial future of borrowers. In order to explore this notion empirically, we examine how incomes have evolved alongside debt over the past two decades.

Discussions of the well-being of borrowers often focus on comparing debt to annual earnings. This is not necessarily incorrect, but since debt measures a "stock" while annual earnings measures a "flow," it can generate misleading results. It would be more useful to compare debt to the "stock" measure of earnings, namely lifetime earnings. Since lifetime earnings are not observable and difficult to estimate, the best approach is to recognize this point when interpreting relationships between earnings and debt.

Among households with outstanding student loan debt, average household wage income increased from just under $43,000 in 1992 to just over $50,000 in 2010, amounting to an increase of $7,411 over this 18-year period. During that same period, the amount of student loan debt taken on by the average household increased from approximately $12,000 to $30,000, amounting to an increase of $18,000. According to these estimates, the increase in student loan debt faced by a typical household (i.e., one facing mean income and mean debt) is more than compensated for with increased earnings over the course of a lifetime. In fact, the increase in earnings received over the course of 2.4 years by a household with earnings at the mean of the distribution would pay for the increase in debt incurred at the mean of the borrowing distribution.

The transitory burden of loan repayment is no greater for today's young workers than it was for young workers two decades ago. If anything, the monthly repayment burden has lessened.

This does not imply that every household with student loan debt in 2010 is necessarily better off than every household with student loan debt in 1992, but the data . . . indicate that the increases in borrowing in the right tail of the distribution were not enormous relative to the increase in mean earnings. For example, the increase in borrowing at the 75th percentile was 2.8 times the increase in mean earnings, and the increase in borrowing at the 90th percentile was 6.4 times the increase in mean earnings. In all cases, it appears that the increase in borrowing would be made up for relatively early in the career of a worker with mean earnings.

The Transient Challenges

Increases in lifetime earnings relative to debt provide a picture of long-run (or "permanent") financial well-being, but may obscure more transient challenges faced by households. For example, an increase in debt may be affordable in the long run but impose monthly payments that squeeze borrowers in the short run, especially early in their careers. We address this question by examining trends in the ratio of monthly payments to monthly income, a comparison of two "flow" measures. . . . Surprisingly, the ratio of monthly payments to monthly income has been flat over the last two decades. Median monthly payments ranged between three and four percent of monthly earnings in every year from 1992 through 2010. Mean monthly payments, which are larger than median payments in each year due to the distribution being right-skewed, declined from 15 percent in 1992 to 7 percent in 2010.

Our analysis suggests that inflation in published tuition prices may account for upward of half of the increase in debt, leaving a significant share of the rise in debt that is unexplained.

We observe the same patterns among households at each percentile in the distribution of payment-to-income ratios and in each category of educational attainment. The ratio of monthly payments to monthly income stayed roughly the same over time, on average, at each percentile and for each education category. By this measure, the transitory burden of loan repayment is no greater for today's young workers than it was for young workers two decades ago. If anything, the monthly repayment burden has lessened.

This surprising finding can be explained in part by a lengthening of average repayment terms during the same period. In 1992, the mean term of repayment was 7.5 years, which increased to 13.4 years in 2010. We suspect that this increase was due primarily to loan consolidation, which increased dramatically in the early 2000s. Loans consolidated with the federal government are eligible for extended repayment terms based on the outstanding balance, with larger debts eligible for longer repayment terms. Average interest rates also declined during this period, which would also lower monthly payments.

The fact that the 90th percentile of the debt-to-income distribution has not grown over the last decades suggests that the outliers featured in media coverage of student loan debt may not be part of a new or growing phenomenon. There is no absolute measure of when a payment-to-income ratio is too high.... We do not find any evidence that the share of borrowers with high payment-to-income ratios has increased consistently over time, with high ratios more common during the 1990s than during the 2000s.

The Reality About Student Loan Debt

The media has provided many anecdotes about recent graduates with large amounts of student loan debt who are in financial distress. Data on the distribution of loan debt, both from the SCF [Survey of Consumer Finances] and other sources, indicate that extremely large debt burdens remain exceptional cases. And large debt burdens are not necessarily an indicator of financial hardship, as they may be used to finance lucrative degrees in business or law. In related work, one of us reported that there is not a strong positive relationship between student debt and various measures of financial hardship, with low-debt households most likely to struggle financially.

Our analysis of the SCF data also provides some initial estimates of the role that different factors have played in driving up student debt over the last two decades. Rising educational attainment explains some of the trend: debt data disaggregated by highest degree earned suggest that graduate education has played a particularly important role, especially for the cases of large debt balances. Better understanding the increase in debt used to finance graduate degrees, which likely vary widely in their economic return, is a ripe subject for future research, as is further exploring the rising debt burdens of individuals who borrowed to attend college but did not complete a degree.

Tuition is also a likely culprit for rising debt, although the limitations of historical data on tuition make it difficult to tell exactly how much of an impact it has had. Our analysis suggests that inflation in published tuition prices may account for upward of half of the increase in debt, leaving a significant share of the rise in debt that is unexplained. Our inability to use net price instead of sticker price means that the importance of tuition is likely overstated, and the unexplained share is probably higher. These facts, coupled with evidence that students are substituting away from paying for college out-of-pocket toward financing, suggest that policy changes, such as lower interest rates and longer loan terms, and behavioral shifts, such as decreased loan aversion, may account for some of the increase in education debt.

We also provide evidence on the evolution of financial well-being of borrowers with student loan debt over the past two decades. Despite the widely held belief that circumstances for borrowers with student loan debt are growing worse over time, our findings reveal no evidence in support of this narrative. In fact, the average growth in lifetime income among households with student loan debt easily exceeds the average growth in debt, suggesting that, all else equal, households with debt today are in a better financial position than households with debt were two decades ago. Furthermore, the incidence of burdensome monthly payments does not appear to have become more widespread over the last two decades.

Future policymaking on student loans should be guided by accurate evidence on the health of the entire market, not atypical anecdotes. The evidence reported above suggests that broad-based policies aimed at all student borrowers, either past or current, are likely to be unnecessary and wasteful given the lack of evidence of widespread financial hardship. Such policies tend to provide the largest benefits to borrowers with the largest debt burdens, who may be the opposite of those most in need. For example, the 2010 SCF indicates that the top quartile of households in terms of income hold 40 percent of outstanding student loan debt.

At the same time, as students take on more debt to go to college, they are taking on more risk. This risk is rewarded for the average borrower with increased earnings, but individuals who make bad or unlucky bets will be farther from financial security than borrowers in the past. This fact highlights the need for robust social safety nets such as income-based repayment and payment deferral for financial hardship, programs which exist but are in need of simplification and improvement. In particular, these programs need to be carefully targeted at borrowers facing significant financial hardship and designed to minimize any perverse incentives such as over-borrowing and tuition inflation.

Private Student Loans Are a Risky Way to Finance College

The Institute for College Access and Success

The Institute for College Access and Success is an independent, nonprofit organization that aims to make higher education more available and affordable for people of all backgrounds.

There has been an increase in private loans coupled with a decrease in borrowers utilizing more affordable federal loans. In addition, private loan borrowers disproportionately attend for-profit and private nonprofit colleges, which typically have higher costs than public two-year and four-year institutions.

Private loans are one of the riskiest ways to finance a college education. Like credit cards, they typically have variable interest rates. Both variable and fixed rates are higher for those who can least afford them—as high as 13% in June 2014. Private loans are not eligible for the important deferment, income-based repayment, or loan forgiveness options that come with federal student loans. Private loans are also much harder than other forms of consumer debt to discharge in bankruptcy. . . .

The Increase in Private Loans

Private loan volume is increasing after earlier declines. Private loan volume has been rising since 2010–11. Data show that annual volume peaked at $18.1 billion in 2007–08 before the credit crunch, then decreased to $5.2 billion by 2010–11 before increasing to $5.5 billion in 2011–12 and $6.2 billion in 2012–13.

Almost half of borrowers could be using more affordable federal loans.

Experts agree that students and families should exhaust all of their federal aid options before even considering private loans. However, almost half (47%) of private loan borrowers in 2011–12 borrowed less than they could have in safer federal Stafford loans:

- 19% took out no Stafford loans at all. This includes: 8% did not apply for federal financial aid, and 11% did apply for federal aid (a requirement for Stafford loans) but did not take out a Stafford loan.

- 28% had Stafford loans, but borrowed less than they could have.

Almost 1.4 million undergraduates borrowed private loans in 2011–12.

The Schools Borrowers Attend

Almost half of private loan borrowers attend lower priced schools.

- In 2011–12, almost half (48%) of private loan borrowers attended schools charging $10,000 or less in tuition and fees.

- Although almost half of all private loan borrowers attended lower priced schools, private loan borrowers are disproportionately represented at higher cost schools. In 2011–12, four in 10 (43%) private loan borrowers attended schools that charge tuition and fees above $10,000, while only 19% of all undergraduates attended such schools.

Private loan borrowers disproportionately attend for-profit and private nonprofit colleges. In 2011–12, for-profit colleges and private nonprofit four-year colleges had disproportionate shares of students with private loans.

- Students attending *for-profit* colleges comprised about 13% of all undergraduates, but 25% of those with private loans.

- Students attending *private nonprofit four-year* colleges comprised about 11% of all undergraduates, but 23% of those with private loans.

- The share of all undergraduates attending *public four-year* colleges (28%) was similar to the percentage of private loan borrowers who attend these schools (31%).

- Students attending *public two-year* colleges are least likely to take out private loans: they comprised about 38% of all undergraduates but only 10% of private loan borrowers.

Trends in the Private Loan Market

Almost 1.4 million undergraduates borrowed private loans in 2011–12. According to federal survey data available every four years, 6% of all undergraduates—1,373,000 students—borrowed private loans in 2011–12. This represents a sharp decline from 2007–08, when 14% of undergraduates—2,901,000 students—borrowed private loans as the market peaked before declining with the financial crisis. But the number and share of students borrowing private loans were higher in 2011–12 than in 2003–04, when only 5% of undergraduates—930,000 students—borrowed.

Private loan borrowing by sector in 2011–12:

- At *for-profit* colleges: 12% of students had private loans, down from 40% in 2007–08.

- At *private nonprofit four-year* colleges: 12% of students had private loans, down from 26% in 2007–08.

- At *public four-year* colleges: 7% of students had private loans, down from 14% in 2007–08.

- At *public two-year* colleges: 2% of students had private loans, down from 4% in 2007–08.

Racial/ethnic differences in borrowing that emerged at the height of the private loan market had disappeared by 2011–12. In 2007–08, African Americans were more likely than other groups to take out private loans, in contrast to 2003–04 and 2011–12. There were no substantial differences in students' likelihood of borrowing private loans by race/ethnicity in 2003–04 or 2011–12. Since private loan borrowing rates by race/ethnicity are available only every four years, there are no public data on whether differential rates of borrowing are reappearing as the market expands again.

5

Private Student Loans Are a Critical Part of the Student Loan Market

Diana G. Carew

Diana G. Carew is an economist and director of the Young American Prosperity Project at the Progressive Policy Institute.

The federal government should work with the private student loan lending market rather than seeking to force private lenders out of the sector altogether, simply because a student loan market 100 percent owned by the government is a bad idea and one that could lead to other problems. Rather than blame private lenders for the high interest rates they charge on student loans, policymakers should see this as a warning sign that students are overextended with debt and that the current lending system needs reform.

If you believe the recent blitz of student debt coverage, greedy private lenders and high interest rates are to blame for the economic woes of recent college graduates. Lending at what is seen to be excessively high interest rates, the pressure on private lenders to restructure student loans, even at the expense of public funds, is rising. At the same time, the government is taking concrete actions to squeeze private lenders out of the student loan market. Now Sen. Elizabeth Warren (D-

Mass.) has followed in President [Barack] Obama's footsteps by proposing to peg student loan interest rates to the government's historically low borrowing costs.

Private Student Lending Is Shrinking

Tempting as it may be, attacking private lenders alone will not solve the student debt problem. For one, private student loans are an increasingly small fraction of total outstanding student debt. And while overall student loan defaults have been rising, private student loan defaults have been falling. Second, although not innocent, villianizing private lenders misses the point: outstanding student debt is rising too much too fast. A government-controlled student loan market will not solve the underlying problem that recent college graduates are struggling in today's slow-growth economy.

Making the government the only higher education lender, at subsidized rates, risks turning student lending into a faucet that can't be turned off.

Since the 2008 financial crisis, the Department of Education has essentially taken over the entire student loan market. The federal guarantee program was scrapped, and interest rates on subsidized Stafford loans were "temporarily" cut in half with another extension debate underway. New government student loans increased 40 percent over 2008–2012 while new private loans fell 75 percent, to just $6 billion last year. The government now holds more than 85 percent of the $1 trillion in outstanding student debt. Meanwhile, just three major private lenders remain active in the market.

There's no doubt that subsidized government student loans must be an essential part of higher education funding. College remains the best way to raise incomes, and the government plays an essential role in providing access to higher education for those who are otherwise unable to afford it.

But making the government the only higher education lender, at subsidized rates, risks turning student lending into a faucet that can't be turned off. A government that controls all student lending could eventually be forced to get into the business of controlling today's excessively rising tuitions. That could be a slippery slope the government may not want to slide into.

What the Private Loan Market Is Telling Us

Instead of attacking the bearer of bad news, we should use private market insights to help guide future education policy. Right now the private market is questioning the financial viability of student debt. The student loan asset-backed securities (SLABS) market remains well below pre-crisis levels. The latest bond offering from Sallie Mae, which tied performance to older student debt obligations, was canceled after two weeks. Clearly the market has doubts about the underlying quality of certain classes of student debt. We would be wise to take these doubts seriously.

Part of this private market uncertainty is due to the rising chorus of student debt legislation—nobody wants to invest in an asset that may not make it to maturity.

But that's exactly the point—investors realize young college graduates are struggling to pay off their debt for reasons other than interest rates. Progressive Policy Institute research shows earnings for recent college graduates fell 15 percent—or by $10,000 in annual terms—since 2000. The slow-growth economy of the last decade hit young people harder than other age groups, with many college graduates taking lower-skill jobs for less pay. The private market is signaling that recent college graduates are financially over-extended.

It's easy to attack private lenders for unfairly charging high interest rates at a time when borrowing costs are historically low. But the fact is students are charged higher interest rates because they are not AA+ rated governments. They are borrowers with little to no credit whose repayment is dependent on future earnings, taking out a loan with no collateral. It's not so simple to refinance this debt, public or private, especially if expected future earnings are falling.

Eventually the Obama administration will have to decide if subsidizing the entire student loan market is desirable or sustainable. Until then, it should work with private lenders instead of working to squeeze them out. That includes requiring better communication with borrowers and encouraging more repayment alternatives for private loans. It also includes borrower protections in the form of responsible oversight from the Consumer Financial Protection Bureau. But it should not include showing private lenders the exit.

6

Most Private Student Loan Complaints Involve Repayment Issues

Consumer Financial Protection Bureau

The Consumer Financial Protection Bureau of the US government aims to help consumer finance markets work by making rules more effective and by empowering consumers to take more control over their economic lives.

Most of the complaints received about private student loans involve repayment issues, such as how to avoid default, barriers to getting reduced repayment plans, payment options that are too little or too late, and a catch-22 that requires some borrowers to begin repaying their loans even though they are still enrolled in school.

Since the [Consumer Financial Protection] Bureau began accepting private student loan complaints in March 2012, the largest subset of complaints stem from borrowers seeking to avoid default during a period of financial hardship. Most frequently, borrowers submitting complaints are seeking to modify repayment terms to obtain a payment they can actually afford. While student loan industry participants have stated that they intend to increase the number of programs to assist borrowers, the increasing volume of complaints from borrowers seeking alternative repayment options suggests that lenders and servicers have yet to address the need for loan workouts in a fulsome manner.

Consumer Financial Protection Bureau, "Annual Report of the CFPB Student Loan Ombudsman," October 16, 2014, pp. 10–15. Courtesy of consumerfinance.gov.

The complaints related to loan modification challenges fall into a number of distinct themes, as outlined below.

No Clear Path to Avoid Default

Borrowers report that many private student lenders and servicers do not transparently communicate consistent information on how to avoid default in times of trouble. Consumers have submitted complaints to the Bureau trying to find out if there are options to lower their monthly payment or to get a payment they can afford. Consumer complaints suggest that there is a lack of transparent information on methods to avoid default, potentially due to lenders and servicers not adequately providing information to consumers about available repayment plans or the lack of clear information available on the lender's or servicer's websites and online servicing platforms.

Borrowers frequently complain that despite repeated attempts to request a lower monthly payment, lenders are often unwilling to constructively work with the borrower on a loan modification.

Investigating potential options requires borrowers to contact their lender or servicer to obtain information, and some consumers note they received conflicting information from multiple customer service representatives about eligibility criteria to enroll in alternative repayment programs.

Proactive Outreach from Borrowers Often Unsuccessful

Borrowers submitting complaints quickly sought help, but were usually rebuffed. Many of the complaints handled by the Bureau suggest that a number of borrowers are eager to protect their credit and avoid the consequences of delinquency and default. When these borrowers anticipated that they would be unable to pay, often due to difficulties securing adequate employment, they sought options for a reduced payment plan. But many of these consumers received responses from lenders and servicers that they were unwilling to offer an alternative repayment option for their loans.

As noted earlier, borrowers frequently complain that despite repeated attempts to request a lower monthly payment, lenders are often unwilling to constructively work with the borrower on a loan modification. One borrower who submitted a complaint with the Bureau received a response from her lender, a very large depository institution, noting that it does not currently offer any assistance through alternative repayment options. The institution also responded that she must pay her high monthly payment or default.

Consumers also stated that they need affordable repayment options that allow them to successfully repay their loans without the financial assistance of co-signers or third parties, such as family members. However, many consumers receive responses from their lender or servicer that no reduced payment options are available for their loans and that they should contact their co-signer to submit a payment or the loan will default.

Options Are Too Little, Too Late

When options do exist, they often provide assistance for just a short period of time. Complaints from private student loan borrowers suggest that a more commonly-utilized method to work with borrowers in distress is the use of short-term forbearance options, often for a non-renewable period of three months.

In some cases, borrowers submitting complaints note that these forbearance options are often too short in duration to truly avoid default.

In other cases, lenders and servicers provide options only after the loan is placed in default. In rare cases, borrowers who submitted complaints are offered the option to enroll in a reduced payment program. However, these plans were generally offered only *after* the borrower had defaulted. Some borrowers have noted that if this option had been made available earlier in the process, they could have avoided default altogether.

[Some private lenders require] consumers to pay a fee in order to postpone payments or apply for forbearance.

Even with short-term forbearance options, consumers may experience unusual processing delays, unclear requirements, and unaffordable fees. Consumers report that they are sometimes instructed to complete an application in order to postpone payments due to a financial hardship. We heard from consumers who experienced difficulty in applying to temporarily postpone payments. They described an array of processing delays which then led to missed payments or default before the servicer approved or denied the application.

For example, some consumers reported that they completed an application only to find out later that this benefit is not available for their loans. Some consumers complained that they did not submit payments after completing the application under the belief that no payments were required, only to find out that the application was denied and their account was past due or possibly in default.

We have previously highlighted the practice of requiring consumers to pay a fee in order to postpone payments or apply for forbearance. Consumers continue to complain that lenders may require a "good-faith" payment in order to apply for temporary forbearance programs. These payments can be approximately $50 per loan as a precondition to place the loan in forbearance for a three-month period. Consumers continue to complain that they cannot afford the forbearance fees or their required monthly payment and subsequently default on their loans.

Catch-22 for Continuing School

Many lenders' in-school deferment policies force borrowers to choose between finishing school and repaying a loan. Generally, private student lenders allow a borrower to postpone payments while enrolled in school full-time. However, many lenders limit this benefit to a certain number of months, usually between 48 and 66 months, so long as the borrower remains enrolled in a full-time program. After this period expires, the borrower is required to begin making payments even if the borrower is still enrolled full-time.

Generally, most private student lenders do not offer additional in-school forbearance if the consumer requires additional time to obtain a degree or if the consumer returns to school to obtain a graduate degree. Consumers complain that they are unable to begin making payments while enrolled in school and request additional forbearance in order to complete their program of study. As a result, consumers report that they were sent to collections or defaulted before graduating from school.

7

Student Loans Promote Poor Decisions and Prolong Adolescence

Jackson Toby

Jackson Toby is professor of sociology emeritus at Rutgers University and former director of the Institute for Criminological Research.

The current system of federally guaranteed student loans does not adequately screen college students for their ability to pay back those loans, resulting in a lack of accountability on the part of students and negative economic consequences for the student and society.

As the class of 2013 graduates, massive student-loan defaults loom. Too many loans were given to students without considering their prospects for finding jobs after graduating and being able to repay their debts.

Factors Causing Poor Employment Prospects

Why are many college graduates unable to find positions that enable them to pay off their student loans? Is it simply a sluggish economy that is not generating enough jobs? The official unemployment rate for people in their late teens and post-college years is around 16 percent—twice the national aver-

Jackson Toby, "The Looming Student Loan Crisis," *The American*, May 14, 2013. Reprinted with permission of the American Enterprise Institute, Washington, DC. All rights reserved.

age—but factor in those who have taken lesser jobs than they expected or who have given up looking for work and that figure rises past 25 percent. As *Wall Street Journal* columnist Daniel Henninger summed up satirically with a fictitious self-introduction of a waiter in a posh restaurant, "Hi, I'm Marty and I'll be your waiter for the next 40 years."

But besides the vicissitudes of the labor market, an additional factor contributes to the poor employment prospects of many college graduates. Too many have enrolled in college believing they could have four years of fun and graduate from *any* four-year college after majoring in *any* field—gender studies, sociology, ethnic studies—and obtain well-paying jobs easily. Unfortunately for them, the market for college graduates has changed. Offering a partial remedy, Senator [Ron] Wyden, a Democrat from Oregon, and Senator [Marco] Rubio, a Republican from Florida, have introduced legislation requiring colleges to report the salaries of their graduates who obtain jobs, and this would go some way toward a remedy.

The portfolio of federally guaranteed student loans passed the $1 trillion mark in early 2012, and it continues to grow.

Except for graduates of pre-professional curricula like engineering or pharmacy, employers can afford to be choosey, even for entry-level jobs and internships. Young, inexperienced graduates who majored in liberal arts fields are finding prospective employers are looking for graduates who have taken difficult courses, have internships on their resumes, and have gotten top grades. As a result, some college graduates find jobs quickly and others drift for months and even years, unemployed or employed in jobs that do not require a college education, earning so little that they are compelled to move back with their parents and extend their adolescence. In short, too many students enroll in college without realizing that they must actually *learn* something from the experience; a diploma is not enough. Recruiters are sophisticated enough to distinguish graduates who majored in fun from graduates who took education seriously and had the ability to profit from diligent study.

Failure to carefully scrutinize employment income was one factor that led to the housing bubble. The student-loan program began in 1965, too early for the lessons of the recent mortgage crisis to give forewarning. But now we know. Before making such a large student loan, an applicant's prospects in the job market should be given consideration. Failing to do so invites a high default rate on student loans. The loans are made either by the Department of Education directly or by private financial institutions and guaranteed by the U.S. Treasury. The size of this loan portfolio now exceeds the total credit-card debt of the American population.

Defaults not only increase the national debt and thereby the overall tax burden, they are also particularly damaging to the prospects of students from low-income families, who are more likely to default than students from more affluent backgrounds. Defaulting on their loans makes it more difficult for them to get on the escalator leading to a better life through improved employment opportunities—precisely what the loans were intended to accomplish.

The Consequences: Prolonged Adolescence and Bad Credit

The portfolio of federally guaranteed student loans passed the $1 trillion mark in early 2012, and it continues to grow. The portfolio consists not only of loans for students from low-income families currently in college but also of hundreds of millions of dollars worth of loans taken out by students who graduated from college decades ago or quit before graduating without fully repaying their loans.

Until quite recently, about a third of college graduates didn't have *any* loan indebtedness when they graduated. Some were lucky enough to have had parents or other relatives who financed their higher educations; others went to low-cost community colleges for their first two years before transferring to senior colleges, worked at low-paying jobs, and saved for college expenses. But the proportion of graduating seniors with student-loan debt has been increasing as the cost of college keeps rising. The average four-year college graduate who took out a loan owed $26,600 in 2011, and this does not count college dropouts who incur burdensome debts before giving up. The average unpaid student loan was $23,650 for 2008 graduates and $18,650 for 2004 graduates.

Many students don't consider that the burden of large student loans can be justified only if they have a realistic chance of high future earnings from employment.

One effect of sizeable student loans on graduates is to make it necessary to find a good job quickly. If graduates fail to find good jobs, they are trapped in a prolonged adolescent limbo, burdening their parents economically and delaying the responsibilities of marriage and children. Former students will eventually default on a considerable portion of these loans—a reasonable estimate is 40 percent—or die before paying them off. This means that student debt is likely to be a permanent drain on taxpayers, as defaults add to the ballooning federal debt.

Defaulters suffer too, as their credit standings will be ruined for years. Even some graduates of professional schools discover that they cannot find jobs in the professions they borrowed large amounts of money to train for—and cannot repay their loans. Nine graduates of New York Law School accused their alma mater of misleading them about their postgraduate employment prospects and sued.

Causes of the Student Loan Crisis

Student loans are risky because of two aspects of a trillion-dollar misunderstanding:

1. The failure of many students to understand the difference between grants, such as Pell grants, which are taxpayer gifts awarded to college students who can demonstrate financial need, and loans, which must eventually be repaid—with interest. Contributing to this misunderstanding is that both types of federal financial aid are funneled though campus departments usually called the "Office of Financial Aid." These offices assemble for students a financial "package" covering current college expenses, including parental contributions, student earnings, grants, and loans. The time when repayment of the loans must begin—six months after graduation—is for many students in the almost unimaginable future. Many students don't consider that the burden of large student loans can be justified only if they have a realistic chance of high future earnings from employment.

2. The assumption of most parents and politicians is that higher education is an investment in future careers. Many students regard a college education that way also, but for a large number of them, college is not investment but consumption: four fun-filled years before they have to settle down to a life of adult drudgery. That is why many enroll in courses they hear are easy, fail to do the required reading, and come late to class and leave early when they attend the class at all. For such students, college is a time-out, or in the words of psychiatrist Erik Erikson, a "psychosocial moratorium." Do students, parents, and lawmakers really want students to incur burdensome loans that must be repaid later—or defaulted on—to finance a psychosocial moratorium?

It is not possible to predict precisely which students are likely to repay their loans and how quickly they can do it. But ignoring the likelihood of students being unable to repay their loans invites similar problems to those that contributed to the housing crisis—bankers did not require applicants for mortgage loans to make down payments, have good credit histories, or produce evidence of earnings from employment. Yet the history of banking over many centuries—and the profitability of most banks—attests to the ability of loan officers to distinguish good risks from bad ones.

The question is whether a student loan system that attempts to control the risk of default is better than one that gives loans promiscuously to all college applicants? Voters would probably say that it is.

What the Department of Education does now is give direct loans to every college student who demonstrates financial need, but without examining evidence of academic ability and other criteria of credit-worthiness. From the liberal standpoint, this policy provides crucial educational opportunities to young people from low-income families. Liberals are willing to have taxpayers pay for the higher default rate in exchange for increasing educational opportunities for children from low-income families. They ignore the fact that students from low-income families already receive Pell grants as well as other need-based scholarships that do not require evidence of good credit ratings or superior academic performance. The Pell grant program has been an expensive drain on the budget and continues to grow. In the 2009–10 academic year, Congress appropriated $25.3 billion for Pell grants for 7.74 million American students; in 2010–11 Congress appropriated $32.9 billion for 8.87 million American students; and in 2011–12, Congress appropriated $34.5 billion in grants to 9.4 million college students. However, students also need loans because the cap on Pell grants, $5,550 in 2010–2011 for students from the lowest-income families, does not provide enough money for the rising tuition rates at most colleges and universities.

Congress established a loan program in addition to the grant program because it seemed politically untenable to provide grants large enough to cover the expenses of the millions of students who wanted to attend college. The logic of loans was to give students partial responsibility for the cost of their post-secondary educations. However, because the federal government guarantees repayment of the loans, taxpayers are ultimately responsible.

Three Possible Approaches

The three possible approaches to the student loan problem are as follows:

1. Turn all the loans into grants so that taxpayers rather than students are responsible for repayment.

2. Continue to provide student loans to all students who demonstrate financial need regardless of whether or not many default.

3. Insert a risk-assessment component into student loans that considers credit-worthiness and past academic performance in order to maximize the likelihood of loan repayment and minimize defaults.

The first proposal is unlikely to attract support, given current concerns with budget deficits and the overhang of the large national debt. Under the second proposal, the trillion dollars of student debt that has already accumulated will grow and the defaults will increase. The third proposal is the only way to keep student debt under control. The best argument against it is that some students who would ultimately pay back their loans will not receive them because they don't appear to be good risks to the screeners and, conversely, that some students who look like good risks to the screeners will ultimately default. Of course, in a decentralized system of loan allocation, students denied a loan from one bank might receive it from another. Although mistakes will be made, the question is whether a student loan system that attempts to control the risk of default is better than one that gives loans promiscuously to all college applicants? Voters would probably say that it is. Moreover, attempting to control the risk of student defaults has an important advantage, as I argued at length in the final chapter of my book, *The Lowering of Higher Education in America*: dangling the prospect of obtaining needed student loans before students and their parents will create an incentive for college students and would-be college students to behave more responsibly. They will be more likely to pay attention in class and do assigned reading, less likely to spend weekends drunk or on "recreational" drugs, and less inclined to accumulate a bad credit rating by maxing out their limits on several credit cards. In order to work as a continuing incentive, this assessment of academic prospects and other criteria of credit worthiness should be carried out at the end of every academic year. In short, a side effect of the risk-assessment approach to student loans is to nudge students in the direction of making responsible adult behavior more attractive—even respectable.

Well, why not?

8

Income-Based Repayment Plans Are Not the Solution

William Elliott

William Elliott is an associate professor at the University of Kansas, where he is director of the Assets and Education Initiative, and senior fellow at the New America Foundation.

The overreliance on income-based repayment plans as a solution to student loan debt masks the larger problem of the overreliance by students and parents on student loans. A promising alternative to college debt is to create Child Savings Accounts at birth that can pay for postsecondary education.

There was a time when conventional wisdom said that student debt is not a problem in and of itself—rather, "high" debt of $100,000 or more is the more pressing concern. A recent report from the Federal Reserve Bank of New York highlights just how out of touch that view is. A staggering percentage of Americans do not pay their student debt, no matter how big or small.

The Problem with Income-Based Repayment Plans

Analysis reveals that 34 percent of students with just $5,000 of outstanding debt—hardly "high"—default on their student loans. Student debt imperils far more than just individual borrowers' monthly budgets. It erodes higher education's ability to deliver on the promise that those who have similar abilities and work equally hard will achieve similar outcomes. Unfortunately, the prevailing policy response—Income-Based Repayment (IBR) plans—does not address the core of the problem.

Concern about rising default rates has spurred increasing calls for greater access to IBR plans, which set repayment expectations at 15 percent of the federal student loan borrower's post-college income. Those who do not pay off their loans within 25 years can have their remaining debt forgiven. These features make IBR schemes less a solution to actual problems and more of a sort of self-soothing device for the American people to feel better about loans. Parents and older Americans don't want to see young adults default. Student borrowers want some reassurance that they will be able to pay off their student loans and still feed themselves. Policymakers need to say they're doing *something* on the issue of student debt. In the meantime, the true threat—student indebtedness itself—continues unabated.

We need a truly new direction, one that helps students get to and through college, and prepares them with a solid financial foundation upon joining the workforce.

The [Barack] Obama administration has waged a successful campaign to promote access to IBR plans—estimating in 2010 that $6.6 billion in loans would be repaid through IBR, a number that today has risen to $27 billion. This number is likely to grow even more, thanks to recent changes that have expanded "Pay-As-You-Earn" eligibility, another type of IBR scheme which caps the borrower's monthly payment at about 10 percent of their discretionary income while forgiving their remaining debt after 20 years of making payments.

This is why IBR misses the mark: because it currently doesn't do enough to address one of the key ways student debt may negatively affect young adults, by limiting their ability to accumulate assets. Students with outstanding student debt, even very small amounts, are more likely to postpone accumulating assets as young adults, as recent research shows. IBR plans may even exacerbate this problem by extending the period of students' indebtedness.

An Alternative to the Current Model

Asset accumulation is important, because it positions young adults for significantly improved economic outcomes over their lifetimes—something higher education is supposed to do. The consequences of diverting income to debt repayment instead of asset accumulation may worsen the wealth divide between those who must take on debt to go to college and those who can avoid it.

Rather than a self-soothing mechanism that allows us to maintain the current financial aid model, we need a truly new direction, one that helps students get to and through college, and prepares them with a solid financial foundation upon joining the workforce. We can plan for a different future, one that favors asset empowerment over debt dependency.

What might an asset-empowered future look like? Giving every child a Child's Savings Account would be a good start. These accounts would hold an initial deposit at birth and offer the opportunity for matching funds paid through public funds. Child Savings Accounts would be a critical part of a strategy to foster expectations among very young students that they should receive postsecondary education and equip them early and often with strategies to pay for it. Researchers refer to this as helping kids develop a college-saver identity. All families would be able to save into the accounts, but public investments, like Pell Grants, could be delivered strategically to a kid's account early enough in her academic trajectory to shape achievement and grow into larger balances.

These are admittedly long-term solutions that don't address our increasingly urgent short-term need to help those already saddled with student debt. But, we should not invest in IBR plans with the expectation that they are a "cure"; at best, they are a costly stopgap measure that mask the underlying problem we face, overreliance on student debt. Let it be clear, IBR plans are necessary only because of a growing recognition that student debt places a destructive burden on some young adults that is counter to our view of education as the "great equalizer." Our financial aid system should strengthen the return on a post-secondary degree not weaken it.

It is long past time for public policy to take a dramatic new course. We have to stop thinking about financial aid as only important for influencing access to college, with our only goal being to make sure kids have money to pay for college. We must consider how it impacts preparation for college, access, completion, as well as young adults' long-term financial health. Considered against this more comprehensive metric, it is clear that over use of student loans is a disturbing—even destructive—practice, and maybe just as obvious that IBR should, at best, be seen only as a short-term solution while we address the real underlying problem, overreliance on student debt.

9

The Student Loan System Is an Economic Bubble

Gary Jason

Gary Jason is a senior editor of Liberty *and author of* Dangerous Thoughts: Provocative Writings on Contemporary Issues.

The increase in the number of student loans is much like the mortgage crisis, leading to an economic bubble where tuitions keep rising and school administrators are unaccountable. Debt and default levels on student loans leave ordinary taxpayers to foot the bill for useless college degrees.

For a number of years now, a number of critics of the American system of higher education have rightly insisted that there is a "bubble" in the system, with more and more students running up loans in amounts they will find difficult to pay back. This bubble has been fueled by the federal government's lavish subsidization of the student loan program (which was nationalized four years ago [2008]), in a way similar to how the housing bubble was fueled by government agencies pushing subprime mortgages.

The Negative Consequences of Student Loans

This extensive government largess has produced a number of unintended—though not necessarily unforeseeable—negative consequences. First, it has dramatically driven up the tuition and fees charged by colleges, which in turn has forced more students to take out loans. This should have been easy to foresee, since the agents running the colleges would know that their clients had access to government-backed loans and so would jack up tuition quickly to extract that money.

Second, this flood of money has only encouraged administrative bloat, which in turn has increased college costs with no increase in the quality of education. Again, this should have been foreseeable. The administration would be rationally well-informed about the new honey-pot of taxpayer-backed loans, and the self-interested administrators are the ones who decide where to spend the money, so you don't need to guess where they will (and did) spend it.

There were 218 schools that actually managed to produce students who had three-year default rates of over 30%, and 37 schools that had rates over 40%!

Third, the rising price of college tends to erase the potential returns of a college education for students of only average ability. In effect, like homeowners who refinance their homes only to squander the increased equity, many students are spending more (and borrowing more) of whatever future extra earnings their college educations will bring.

Student Loan Default Rates

Two recent studies suggest that this bubble is indeed real and is beginning to burst. The first is the recent Department of Education report on student loan default rates. The report shows that the two-year default rate rose from 8.8% in FY (fiscal year) 2009 to 9.1% in FY 2010. This marks the fifth year of increases in the two-year default rates—indeed, the two-year rate is nearly double what it was in FY 2005. This means that the number of borrowers whose first payments were due between 10/01/2009 and 9/30/2010 and who defaulted before 09/30/2011 went up dramatically—numbering 375,000 in all, on a base of 4.1 million borrowers entering repayment. Remember—all these loans are ultimately guaranteed by the government.

The FY 2009 three-year default rates—which the Department views as more indicative of ultimate defaults—was 13.4%, essentially the same as the 13.8% for the FY 2008 cohort. In private non-profit institutions, the three-year default rate was 7.5%, at public institutions it was 11%, and at private for-profit colleges it hit 22.7%.

There were 218 schools that actually managed to produce students who had three-year default rates of over 30%, and 37 schools that had rates over 40%!

As bad as these stats are, remember that they do not count borrowers who were allowed to postpone payments due to unemployment or other hardships.

Given that over half of all recent college grads are unemployed (or employed only at jobs not requiring a college education), we can expect those default rates to rapidly rise.

Rising Student Debt Levels

The second study is the Pew Research Center's report on student debt levels. It notes that in 2010, fully 19% (i.e., nearly one fifth) of American households had student loan debt, which is up considerably from the 15% level that obtained in 2007 and is more than double the percentage that obtained in 1990.

The percentage of households headed by someone younger than 35 that had student loan debt is an astounding 40%.

Compared to other household debts (such as for automobiles, credit cards, installment loans, and mortgages), student loan debt is still minor. It is only 5% of all household debt as of 2010. But this is not quite comforting, because just three years ago it was only 3% of all debts, and worse, unlike the other forms of debt, taxpayer-backed student loans are not dischargeable in bankruptcy.

The Pew Study also reports other unpleasant news. First, the average outstanding student loan balance is growing rapidly—up 14% from $23,349 in 2007 to $26,682 in 2010. And those most deeply in debt are getting deeper in the hole: while 10% of debtors in 2007 owed more than $54,238, 10% of debtors in 2010 owed more than $61,894 (in constant 2011 dollars).

Second, the amount of student loan debt relative to other household income or assets is highest among households at the bottom fifth of the income scale.

In fine, the student loan program, meaning the use of taxpayer guarantees to fuel the rapid growth in college loans, has been a textbook illustration of moral hazard. It has induced often marginal students to rack up debts to get often marginal degrees (or none at all), and has induced colleges to expand often pointless administration and useless programs (victims studies, anyone?).

Remember, under recently adopted rules, payment on student loans will be capped at only 10% of the borrower's "discretionary" income, and the balance "forgiven" after twenty years. What this means is that more and more massive amounts of bad student loan debt will be saddled on the backs of taxpayers, *many of whom never got to go to college in the first place!*

This is a program that desperately needs reform before it simply melts down—like the mortgage market did not long ago.

10

Students Should Refuse to Pay Back Student Loans in Protest

Kyle Schmidlin

Kyle Schmidlin is a writer and musician living in Austin, Texas, who operates Third Rail News.

Something radical needs to be done about the amount of debt held by Americans, and holders of student loan debt ought to take collective action and refuse to pay back their loans. Americans need to stand together and refuse the oppression of debt.

R ecently, news broke that Rolling Jubilee, a nonprofit organization dedicated to the eradication of debt, purchased $4 million in private student loan debt and forgave all of it, alleviating some 2,000 Americans of that oppressive burden. The group purchased the loans for pennies on the dollar from the notorious for-profit Everest College. And it's only the beginning—according to Rolling Jubilee's website, they've forgiven more than $18.5 million in debt, much of it medical, on only $701,000 raised.

The Problem of American Debt

Such activism cannot be praised enough. It's entirely selfless, brings important issues to light, and directly aids many Americans. But it can only go so far. The total national debt, both public and private, is a preposterous $60 trillion. If Rolling Jubilee succeeded in wiping out $4 million of that total every day, it'd take more than 41,000 years for America to be debt-free. Even if they focused only on, say, mortgages, it'd take over 9,000 years.

Of course, a lot more than $4 million moves through the American economy every day. But the numbers still help illustrate the obvious: something much more radical has to be done, a fact which Rolling Jubilee organizer Astra Taylor concedes. In a recent *New Yorker* profile, Taylor said, "We shouldn't have to buy this debt. It's treating a symptom without ever treating the disease."

To slap such exorbitant debt on new graduates, especially in this economy, is an aggressive undermining of human rights.

The problem of debt is far beyond the scope of any one person or organization to take care of. Acting *en masse*, however, there is a great deal Americans can do. The best solution to the student loan crisis is a very elegant and simple one: stage a collective refusal to make good on student loan debt. Such a boycotting of payments is well within the power, not to mention the rights, of the American citizenry, and it makes good sense to take such a collective action.

The Refusal to Pay

In the past, activists have resisted paying taxes on the basis of disagreement with government policies. Among the signatories of a 1968 refusal to pay a Vietnam War tax were Noam Chomsky, Howard Zinn and Gloria Steinem, but the practice dates back centuries—Jesus's famous "Render unto Caesar" quote relates to the idea. Refusing to pay student loan debt is a similar form of resistance.

The total national student loan debt is more than $1.2 trillion, the bulk of which—about $1 trillion—is owed by students to the federal government. According to a 2013 study, the average debt held by a graduate in 2012 was almost $30,000. Forty million young Americans are saddled with this burden and 7 million of them have defaulted already.

To slap such exorbitant debt on new graduates, especially in this economy, is an aggressive undermining of human rights. And the punishment for not paying, for those who either can't find work or are courageous enough to pursue their dreams despite their debt, can be severe: ruined credit, wage garnishment (for those lucky enough to have wages), vicious harassment from collectors, and enormous fees as collection of the debt is outsourced to private entities. All of this effectively penalizes poverty. With such immense pressure funneling millions of graduates into whatever menial job they can find in order to begin making payments, student loan debt can't be regarded as anything other than a modern form of indentured servitude.

The Government's Solution

And there is no indication that help is forthcoming from Washington. For all his talk and campaign promises, the most President [Barack] Obama has done to offer relief is to lower interest rates from 6.8 percent to 4.66 percent, a paltry offering that will be all but undone as the rates go back up over the next couple of years. Meanwhile, the Department of Education outsources a great deal of its debt collection to private companies that aggressively bully, intimidate, harass and lie to consumers in an attempt to retrieve the money. Far from helping, this "government of the people" has sent the most bloodthirsty financial bulldogs from the corporate sector after their own weary, broke citizens.

Worse, tuition costs continue to soar even as the degree itself becomes, arguably, much less valuable. The market is so saturated with college graduates that the girl making your coffee just might have a master's in sociology. More tuition dollars than ever go toward covering the costs of bloated university administrations and ever-more grandiose college sports programs and arenas.

Nothing could send a stronger message than 40 million indebted graduates standing together in a boycott of student loan payments.

Websites like the empathetically named youcandealwithit .com, closely affiliated with the federal government's student loan program, offer helpful suggestions like, "Take a look at what you have or want and determine what you can't live without. As hard as it is, you may need to give some things up." Some of what they suggest living without includes a car, a computer, a cell phone, pets and entertainment. Just be a working, sleeping and eating drone—whatever it takes to pay that debt.

The Congressional Budget Office recently reported that over the next ten years, the federal government will make an astounding $127 billion in profit off of student loans. Thousands of lucrative organizations exist for the sole purpose of extracting money from Middle America, for-profit colleges and debt collectors chief among them. The very practice of buying a debt at a reduced price and then collecting the full amount is one of the most unconscionably immoral crimes that can even be imagined—it's pure corporate piracy with no community benefit whatsoever.

Shifting the Balance of Power

Student loans provide an easy avenue for resistance. Not paying them would be like taking back the bailout money the government gave bankers and other financial criminals in 2009. The dollar amounts aren't far off, and if American tax dollars can be used for a CEO's bonus they can damn sure be used for education. It happens one way and not the other because the moneyed CEO can influence policy in a way ordinary Americans can't. The balance of power can be shifted, but only by collective action. Nothing could send a stronger message than 40 million indebted graduates standing together in a boycott of student loan payments.

Any number of things can happen after that. Perhaps Americans will demand the right to pay back their debts on their own terms rather than those imposed by collection agencies and the Department of Education. Perhaps they won't pay anything back at all. There will be backlash from powerful institutions, but those challenges can be overcome.

Waiting for a debt solution from above is not an option. There is simply no motivation for the government or private businesses to reduce the debt Americans owe—they can collect on it until the end of time. It is incumbent on Americans to resist debt, up to and including, if possible, refusal to pay. Just as laborers, suffragists and civil rights advocates rallied for equal rights and fair treatment, debtors must come together and unite with a singular purpose. Rolling Jubilee and Strike Debt have championed the charge for economic justice, both in outlining principles and taking action. All of the 99 percent should join them, whether their debt is from medical expenses, student loans or mortgages.

America has the resources to instate healthcare, education and a home as inalienable human rights. It's a paradisiacal potential we run the risk of squandering every day we voluntarily admit our bondage to debt. There is no realistic way for Americans to climb out of this hole other than by standing together and refusing to allow the oppression to continue.

11

Student Loan Eligibility Should Be Restricted to the Most Needy

Richard Vedder

Richard Vedder is Distinguished Professor of Economics at Ohio University in Athens, Ohio.

There are as many college-degree holders as those with student loan debt and many debt holders will never be able to pay back their loans, even as they age. Thus, student loans should be constrained, only going to the neediest students and in lower amounts.

Here is arguably the most startling statistic you have heard this year: *It is likely that there are at least as many adult Americans with student-loan debts outstanding as there are living bachelor's degree recipients who ever took out student loans.* That's right: as many debtors as degree holders! How can that be? First, huge numbers of those borrowing money *never* graduate from college. Second, many who borrow are not in baccalaureate degree programs. Three, people take forever to pay their loans back.

The Burden of Student Loan Debt

Let's do the math. Recent data suggest there are about 40 million holders of student-loan debt. The New York Fed [Federal Reserve Bank of New York] in a study puts the number a little lower, but estimates by the Consumer Financial Protection Bureau (CFPB) suggest a somewhat higher figure. There are, give or take a million, roughly 60 million college graduates. Yet a good proportion, somewhere around one-third, of college graduates, never borrowed money to go to college (that is probably doubly true of graduates in the early 1990s). In other words, at most 40 million adults with four-year degrees borrowed money. Bottom line: an awful lot of people borrow to go to college and never graduate, and/or take forever to pay off their student loans.

It seems highly likely that a very significant portion of total [student loan] obligations—maybe over one-third—is held by individuals with incomes less than their debt obligation.

Before getting to the Fed study, I think individuals risk being over their head when their loan debt exceeds their annual income. Take a former student with a $50,000 debt with a $40,000 income. While the future interest rate on student loans is uncertain let us assume one of 5 percent, lower than what the law for the next fiscal year requires but more than President [Barack] Obama wants. A person with a $40,000 income might have only $28,000 of what the Feds define as discretionary income. Devoting 10 percent of that income to debt servicing (the maximum required under an executive order), a debtor would pay $2,800 annually in debt service, $2,500 of which would go for interest, and only $300 for principal. Since federal policy puts a 20-year time limit on repayment, and it is likely it might take more than 20 years to repay the loan, it likely will never be fully repaid—the government will take a hit. When the debt-income ratio is under one, that is much less likely to occur. My wife, a retired guidance counselor, talked to a former student of hers recently with a six-digit debt incurred while in undergraduate and law school that is perhaps three times her income, and she literally has health problems from worrying about the crushing burden. This is not rare these days.

The Federal Reserve study of federal student loan debt deserves more attention than it has received. It tells a mostly grim story. First the "good" news. It is true that statistics on average debt loads (now approaching $25,000) overstate what most lenders owe. The median debt, as of 2011, was closer to $13,000, a manageable burden for the vast majority of borrowers. Only 28 percent of borrowers owe $25,000 or more in debt.

But the good news morphs quickly into bad news. Although most debtors owe relatively manageable amounts, it is not true that most of the debt is held by persons with modest debt obligations. Indeed, it appears that about two-thirds of the debt relates to loans of $25,000 or more per person. Moreover, it appears well over 40 percent of the $870-billion in debt (the CFPB says over $1-trillion) is held by those with very large burdens—$50,000 a year or more. While we do not know debt-income ratios for borrowers, it seems highly likely that a very significant portion of total obligations—maybe over one-third—is held by individuals with incomes less than their debt obligation. If this debt were held by private banks without any federal guarantees, we would be talking about hundreds of billions of dollars in problem loans—a potential serious drag on financial institutions even now recovering from the financial crisis.

The Real Problem

It gets worse. Statistics on nonpayers, delinquent payers, those in default, etc., tend to understate the real problem—by important magnitudes. Many borrowers are not classified as not paying on their loans because of special provisions in the law that have delayed the beginning of repayment. Not only do borrowers not have to pay loans back while in school, they even get a grace period after graduation before payments start coming due. If we classify those persons, correctly, as not making loan repayments, the percentage of borrowers with payment problems rises sharply, from about 12 or so percent to well over 20 percent—a very high proportion.

Moreover, this debt is not all held by young persons who face a likely upward trajectory in their earnings over time. Roughly 40 percent of borrowers are over 40, and many even are over 50—people hoping to retire in another decade or so. The median age of debt holders appears to be about 34, an age when many of us think borrowers should have about finished paying off their student loans.

We need to selectively wean college students from their debt addiction by beginning to restrict eligibility for borrowing to the most needy. We need to constrain the amounts borrowed more than at present. We need to reduce an already significant federal unfunded liability. One positive by-product would almost certainly be a sharp reduction in the explosion in tuition costs.

12

A Third Way Past Student Loans

David N. Bass

David N. Bass is communications director and grants officer for the John William Pope Foundation, an independent grant-making organization.

A solution to the problem of excessive student loans is to direct young people away from traditional four-year schools into vocational-oriented training. The apprenticeship model can be a win-win for both students, who get a free education, and corporations, who get skilled workers.

As lawmakers debate various proposals to ostensibly solve the $1 trillion student-loan crises in America—lower student-loan interest rates or forgive loans altogether being two—clear-thinking individuals should catch a vision for alternatives.

In two decades, imagine a post-secondary education arena in which a majority of students avoid the need for student loans in the first place. Or, if loans are necessary, have a job upon graduation sufficient to pay them off. Novel concepts? Perhaps. But they shouldn't be.

We are witnessing the result of excessive student loan consumption by the predicament of the Millennial generation— roughly those born between 1980 and 2000. Despite an improving economy, many of these young people remain at

David N. Bass, "A Third Way Past Student Loans," *American Spectator*, March 31, 2015. spectator.org. Copyright © 2015 American Spectator. All rights reserved. Reproduced with permission.

home, lacking true financial independence, delaying marriage, and putting off having children. One of the biggest culprits, if not *the* biggest, is student loan debt.

Too often, the solutions preferred focus on either further subsidizing an increasingly low return-on-investment [ROI] college education or winking at students' loan obligations. There is a better way—putting more emphasis on directing young people away from traditional four-year schools (and what might end up being an expensive and low-ROI degree) and toward more vocational-oriented training.

The combination of an associates degree and practical experience in an in-demand field could actually result in more financial stability and well-being for a young person than a four-year liberal arts degree.

From a practical standpoint, education should have as a central goal the acquisition of skills and knowledge demanded by the marketplace. This goal is accomplished for many young people through a traditional four-year route, but for many others, such as those from low-income families, that option is not always feasible. Alternatives are needed.

Thinkers have caught on to this, but solutions are too-oft ignored by many advisors. "Americans have a host of postsecondary options other than a four-year degrees—associate degrees, occupational certificates, industry certifications, apprenticeships," writes Tamara Jacobs in the *Wall Street Journal*. "Many economists are bullish about the prospects of what they call 'middle-skilled' workers. In coming years, according to some, at least a third and perhaps closer to half of all U.S. jobs will require more than high school but less than four years of college—and most will involve some sort of technical or practical training."

It seems counter-intuitive, but the combination of an associates degree and practical experience in an in-demand field could actually result in more financial stability and well-being for a young person than a four-year liberal arts degree. In fact, increasingly, it's becoming the norm.

One of the best ways to achieve this is through apprenticeships. A fine example exists in North Carolina right now. The NC Triangle Apprenticeship Program (NCTAP), operating in the Raleigh area of North Carolina, is a hands-on, intensive technical experience that actually prepares high-school students for existing jobs and a successful career. NCTAP was born out of a desire for students with an engineering bent at Thales Academy (a local network of private schools covered in this [*American Spectator*] magazine here) to have an apprenticeship opportunity.

Prospective participants apply for NCTAP early in their high-school career. The program begins during their sophomore year and continues for four full years—through the completion of an associates degree in mechanical engineering technology at a local community college. The program has the added benefit of encouraging young people to get serious about a career trajectory early on, rather than as a thirty-something still living in mom's basement.

The end result—a skilled worker—is a worthwhile investment for any business.

While enrolled in school, students participate in an apprenticeship at a number of high-caliber local businesses, including the pharmaceutical giant GlaxoSmithKline and the kitchen ventilation company CaptiveAire. The one-two punch of a two-year degree mixed with invaluable on-the-job experience can't be underscored enough. In a job market saturated with bachelor degree recipients, one of the most defining characteristics to set apart applicants is actual experience—and far better, actual experience in a given field of specialization. NCTAP provides it.

65

"By the time students have finished their apprenticeship and associates degree, they already have three to four years of work seniority—and no debt," says NCTAP chairman Lukas Schoenwetter. "They can make a very good living and climb the career ladder fast."

Another kicker: The associates degree is entirely paid for by the employer. So completers of the program have zero debt. Imagine the life of success created by this pathway: a practical, technical degree mixed with practical, technical training—with no debt upon graduation. That is a rosy picture for a 20-year-old just beginning a career. Even if NCTAP apprentices choose to return to obtain a four-year degree, they will be in a much better position to do so in a financially prudent way.

Who shoulders the cost for the apprenticeship? The companies involved. But the end result—a skilled worker—is a worthwhile investment for any business.

"The real cost to our partner companies is the pay and benefits for apprentices over the four-year duration of the program, plus approximately $5,000 for the associates degree in mechanical engineering," says Kent Misegades, vice chairman of NCTAP and an engineer by trade. That estimated cost is $140,000 total for each participant. But as Misegades notes, "These are productive employees and worth every penny."

The big news is that, in each case, a job awaits young people upon graduation from the program. "Virtually 100 percent of those who make it through the program will be hired by their employer," Misegades notes.

NCTAP is a model that specifically targets high-achieving students, but the same approach could be taken with strugglers or those from low-income backgrounds.

U.S. Department of Labor Secretary Thomas Perez recently visited NCTAP and called it a model for the nation to follow.

"Apprenticeships give participants a very structured learning and training environment and also provides employers the opportunity to grow talent locally," says Schoenwetter. "Good apprentices will pay back the investment of an employer at the end of three to four years."

This model is a win-win for both students and corporations. It deserves more attention, primarily because such approaches threaten the established university network that benefits from bloated costs and readily available student loan commitments at exorbitant amounts, factors that stall the career growth of young people.

This approach doesn't help current youth mired in student-loan obligations. But it is a vision for the future that we should be encouraging now. As many observers begin to predict a coming collapse of the so-called "higher education bubble," apprenticeship examples such as NCTAP will get more attention. And deservedly so.

Organizations to Contact

The editors have compiled the following list of organizations concerned with the issues debated in this book. The descriptions are derived from materials provided by the organizations. All have publications or information available for interested readers. The list was compiled on the date of publication of the present volume; the information provided here may change. Be aware that many organizations take several weeks or longer to respond to inquiries, so allow as much time as possible.

American Student Assistance
100 Cambridge St., Suite 1600, Boston, MA   02114
(800) 999-9080
e-mail: information@asa.org
website: www.asa.org

American Student Assistance is a private nonprofit dedicated to opening the gateway to opportunity by revolutionizing the way students approach, finance, and repay their higher education costs. American Student Assistance provides student loan education and the development of financial competencies through the use of innovative web-based tools and neutral advice—all free of charge to students and alumni. American Student Assistance has a variety of publications for students, parents, counselors, and the media, all available at its website.

Brookings Institution
1775 Massachusetts Ave. NW, Washington, DC   20036
(202) 797-6000
e-mail: communications@brookings.edu
website: www.brookings.edu

The Brookings Institution is a nonprofit public policy organization that conducts independent research. The institution uses its research to provide recommendations that advance the goals of strengthening American democracy, fostering social welfare and security, and securing a cooperative international system. The Brookings Institution publishes a variety of research through the Brown Center on Education Policy, including a recent report titled "Are College Students Borrowing Blindly?"

Center for College Affordability and Productivity (CCAP)
1055 Thomas Jefferson St. NW, Suite L 26
Washington, DC 20007
(202) 621-0536
e-mail: theccap@gmail.com
website: www.centerforcollegeaffordability.org

The Center for College Affordability and Productivity (CCAP) is dedicated to researching the rising costs and stagnant efficiency in higher education, with special emphasis on the United States. CCAP seeks to facilitate a broader dialogue on the issues and problems facing the institutions of higher education with the public, policy makers, and the higher education community. CCAP publishes a blog and a variety of policy papers, including "Dollars, Cents, and Nonsense: The Harmful Effects of Federal Student Aid."

The Heritage Foundation
214 Massachusetts Ave. NE, Washington, DC 20002-4999
(202) 546-4400 • fax: (202) 546-8328
e-mail: info@heritage.org
website: www.heritage.org

The Heritage Foundation is a conservative public policy organization dedicated to promoting policies that align with the principles of free enterprise, limited government, individual freedom, traditional American values, and a strong national defense. The Heritage Foundation conducts research on policy issues for members of Congress, key congressional staff members, policy makers in the executive branch, the nation's news media, and the academic and policy communities. The foundation has hundreds of reports, fact sheets, testimonies, and commentaries available at its website.

The Institute for College Access and Success (TICAS)

405 14th St., Suite 1100, Oakland, CA   94612
(510) 318-7900 • fax: (510) 318-7918
website: www.ticas.org

The Institute for College Access and Success (TICAS) works to make higher education more available and affordable for people of all backgrounds. TICAS conducts and supports nonpartisan research, analysis, and advocacy. TICAS has a variety of reports available at its website, such as "Student Debt and the Class of 2013."

Institute for Higher Education Policy (IHEP)

1825 K St. NW, Suite 720, Washington, DC   20006
(202) 861-8223 • fax: (202) 861-9307
e-mail: institute@ihep.org
website: www.ihep.org

The Institute for Higher Education Policy (IHEP) is a nonpartisan, nonprofit organization committed to promoting access to and success in higher education for all students. IHEP is committed to equality of opportunity for all and helps low-income, minority, and other historically underrepresented populations gain access to and achieve success in higher education. IHEP aims to enhance college affordability by reshaping college finance systems and publishes reports such as "Making Sense of the System: Financial Aid Reform for the 21st Century Student."

National Education Association (NEA)

1201 16th St. NW, Washington, DC   20036-3290
(202) 833-4000 • fax: (202) 822-7974
website: www.nea.org

The National Education Association (NEA) is an educator membership organization that works to advance the rights of educators and children. NEA focuses its energy on improving the quality of teaching, increasing student achievement, and making schools safe places to learn. NEA also concentrates on issues of higher education, and within its Degrees Not Debt Campaign are a variety of media on the issue of student loans.

New America Foundation
1899 L St. NW, Suite 400, Washington, DC 20036
(202) 986-2700 • fax: (202) 986-3696
website: www.newamerica.org

The New America Foundation is a nonprofit, nonpartisan public policy institute that invests in new thinkers and new ideas to address the next generation of challenges facing the United States. The Foundation's Postsecondary National Policy Institute serves as a source of professional development for congressional staff working on higher education issues. Among the many publications available at its website is the primer "Federal Student Aid: A Background Primer."

Progressive Policy Institute (PPI)
1200 New Hampshire Ave. NW, Suite 575
Washington, DC 20036
(202) 525-3926 • fax: (202) 525-3941
website: www.ppionline.org

The Progressive Policy Institute (PPI) is a nonprofit organization that works to advance progressive, market-friendly ideas that promote American innovation, economic growth, and wider opportunity. PPI focuses on the four main areas of competitiveness, energy, medical innovation, and housing and financial services. Numerous articles can be found on the PPI website, including such titles as "Why Student Debt Proposals in Congress Are only a Band-Aid."

US Department of Education
400 Maryland Ave. SW, Washington, DC 20202
(800) 872-5327
website: www.ed.gov

The US Department of Education was established with the goal of improving education nationwide through the use of federally mandated education programs. The executive agency

71

manages the Federal Student Aid office. Its website has a variety of publications on student loans and administers the *FAFSA,* or *Free Application for Federal Student Aid.*

Bibliography

Books

Joel Best and Eric Best — *The Student Loan Mess: How Good Intentions Created a Trillion-Dollar Problem.* Berkeley: University of California Press, 2014.

Bruce Chapman, Timothy Higgins, and Joseph E. Stiglitz, eds. — *Income Contingent Loans: Theory, Practice, and Prospects.* New York: Palgrave Macmillan, 2014.

Alan Collinge — *The Student Loan Scam: The Most Oppressive Debt in US History, and How We Can Fight Back.* Boston: Beacon Press, 2009.

Dorothy B. Durband and Sonya L. Britt, eds. — *Student Financial Literacy: Campus-Based Program Development.* New York: Springer, 2012.

Marcel Gérard and Silke Uebelmesser, eds. — *The Mobility of Students and the Highly Skilled: Implications for Education Financing and Economic Policy.* Cambridge, MA: MIT Press, 2014.

Brad J. Hershbein and Kevin M. Hollenbeck, eds. — *Student Loans and the Dynamics of Debt.* Kalamazoo, MI: Upjohn Institute, 2015.

Natalie E. Jelinek and Victoria S. Leroy, eds. — *Federal Student Loans and Pell Grants: Terms, Conditions, and Analysis.* New York: Nova Science Publishers, 2011.

D. Bruce Johnstone and Pamela N. Marcucci	*Financing Higher Education Worldwide: Who Pays? Who Should Pay?* Baltimore, MD: Johns Hopkins University Press, 2010.
Anya Kamenetz	*How Our Future Was Sold Out for Student Loans, Credit Cards, Bad Jobs, No Benefits, and Tax Cuts for Rich Geezers—and How to Fight Back.* New York: Riverhead Books, 2007.
Lynnette Khalfani	*Zero Debt for College Grads: From Student Loans to Financial Freedom.* New York: Kaplan, 2007.
Suzanne Mettler	*Degrees of Inequality: How the Politics of Higher Education Sabotaged the American Dream.* New York: Basic Books, 2014.
Christine Romans	*Smart Is the New Rich: Money Guide for Millennials.* Hoboken, NJ: John Wiley & Sons, 2015.
SALT	*The Military Smartbook for Defeating Student Debt.* Boston: American Student Assistance, 2014.
Dave Smith	*College Without Student Loans: Attend Your Ideal College & Make It Affordable Regardless of Your Income.* New York: Morgan James Publishing, 2013.
Gen Tanabe and Kelly Tanabe	*1001 Ways to Pay for College: Strategies to Maximize Financial Aid, Scholarships, and Grants.* Belmont, CA: SuperCollege, 2015.

Periodicals and Internet Sources

Bob Adelmann — "Student Loan Consequences: Real, Costly, and Personal," *New American*, January 29, 2013.

Beth Akers — "The Typical Household with Student Loan Debt," *The Brown Center Chalkboard*, June 19, 2014. www.brookings.edu.

Beth Akers and Matthew M. Chingos — "Are College Students Borrowing Blindly?," Brookings Institution, December 10, 2014. www.brookings.edu.

Jill Barshay — "Measuring the Cost of Federal Student Loans to Taxpayers," *Washington Monthly*, June 16, 2014.

Stephen Burd — "Getting Rid of the College Loan Repo Man," *Washington Monthly*, September/October 2012.

Lindsey Burke — "Elizabeth Warren Leaves Taxpayers on Hook for More Student Loan Subsidies," *Washington Times*, June 9, 2014.

Paul Campos — "Student Loans: The Next Housing Bubble," *Salon*, February 4, 2013. www.salon.com.

Melissa Clyne — "Americans Go Back to School Just to Get Cheap Student Loans," *Newsmax*, March 3, 2014. www.newsmax.com.

Chris Denhart   "How the $1.2 Trillion College Debt
                 Crisis Is Crippling Students, Parents
                 and the Economy," *Forbes*, August 7,
                 2013.

Susan Dynarski   "Loans for Educational Opportunity:
and Daniel   Making Borrowing Work for Today's
Kreisman   Students," The Hamilton Project,
                 October 2013. www.hamiltonproject
                 .org.

William Gale and "Should Taxpayers Rescue
Benjamin Harris Debt-Stressed College Grads?,"
                 Fortune, June 11, 2014.

William G. Gale "Student Loans Rising," Tax Policy
et al.   Center, May 2014.
                 www.brookings.edu.

Gloria Goodale   "Student Loans: Is Petition to Forgive
                 Debt Completely a Good Idea?,"
                 Christian Science Monitor, April 20,
                 2012.

Robert Gordon   "Extending Lower Student-Loan
                 Interest Rates Is Not the Answer,"
                 New Republic, June 11, 2013.

Michael   "Rising Student Debt Burdens:
Greenstone and   Factors Behind the Phenomenon,"
Adam Looney   The Hamilton Project, July 2013.
                 www.hamiltonproject.org.

Elahe Izadi   "Student Loans: It's a Women's
                 Issue," *National Journal*, June 5, 2014.

Andrew Kelly and "The Democrats' Student-Loan
Kevin James   Weapon," *Wall Street Journal*,
                 September 17, 2014.

Megan McArdle "Stop Giving Everyone a Student Loan," *Bloomberg*, March 31, 2015. www.bloomberg.com.

Neal McCluskey "Student Loans: From Completely Disastrous, to Just 99 Percent," *Cato at Liberty*, May 22, 2013. www.cato.org.

Daniel Oliver "Hey, Hey, Ho, Ho, Student Debt Has Got to Go!," *Federalist*, May 8, 2014. www.thefederalist.com.

Sophie Quinton "The Problem with Student-Loan Forgiveness," *National Journal*, April 21, 2014.

Jason Richwine "The Unknown Cost of Federal Student Loans," *Issue Brief*, no. 3923, April 24, 2013. www.heritage.org.

Charles Scaliger "Are the Feds Reaping Windfall Profits from Student Loans?," *New American*, November 30, 2013.

Joe Valenti and David A. Bergeron "How Qualified Student Loans Could Protect Borrowers and Taxpayers," Center for American Progress, August 20, 2013. www.americanprogress.org.

Richard Vedder, Christopher Denhart, and Joseph Hartge "Dollars, Cents, and Nonsense: The Harmful Effects of Federal Student Aid," Center for College Affordability and Productivity, June 2014. www.centerforcollegeaffordability.org.

Mitchell D. Weiss "5 Things We Can Do Now to Solve the Student Loan Problem," *Money*, April 8, 2015.

Kevin D.
Williamson

"Student-Loan Default Is Not a
Moral Good," *National Review
Online*, February 25, 2015.
www.nationalreview.com.

Index